GOD MADE THE ANGELS

This story is about lots and lots of Angels. God made them, bright and beautiful, out of nothing at all!

NOW LET'S think way, way back, before the world was made. There was no one but God, the Blessed Trinity. God was very, very happy. God said, "I am so happy, so I want to make someone else happy. I want to be good to someone else." So God thought and said, "Let's make some Angels." God made many, many Angels. God made them a little like Himself. Angels are spirits and have no bodies. But we draw pictures of them with bodies to help us think about them.

WHEN MRS. FINLEY makes an apple pie, she needs apples and flour and sugar and butter and milk and cinnamon and nutmeg. Sometimes she uses a pie mix or buys the pie at the bakery, but then the *baker* had to use all of these things. *Nobody* can make a pie out of nothing at all!

SUGAR

WHEN DAD helped Ned make his wagon, they needed wheels and rods and wood and nails and a hammer and paint. *Nobody* can make a wagon out of nothing at all. No matter what we make, we always need something to make it out of. But with God it is different. God makes things out of nothing at all.

GOD SIMPLY SAID, "Let's make some Angels," and there they were, lots and lots of Angels. They were all beautiful and smart. God had made them out of nothing at all. In the beginning, the Angels could not see God. Before they could see God they had to pass a test. They lined up for the test with their leaders, Michael and Lucifer. These were two specially bright and beautiful Angels, called Archangels. God said, "Will you do what I want?" That was the test.

MICHAEL the Archangel bowed low before God. "O Lord God Almighty, I will do anything You want!" he said. Lots and lots of Angels followed Michael. They gave a great shout: "We will do anything You want, Lord God Almighty!"

But where was Lucifer? What was he saying?

LUCIFER was shining very brightly; that is what his name means–the bright and shining one. He thought, "I'm too bright and smart to bow down before anyone. I'm just as good as God is." So he cried out, "No! I won't do what You want. I will not serve!" And a big crowd of Angels shouted with him: "I will not serve! I will not serve!"

THAT STARTED a great fight. Michael and his good Angels were horrified! "So you think you are as good as God is! You are all wrong! Who is like God? No one!"

Michael and his Angels couldn't bear to see Lucifer and his Angels disobeying God. They fought and fought. And the good Angels won. Lucifer and his crowd of bad Angels were all thrown out of Heaven.

WHEN ANGELS make up their minds, they can never change. When Lucifer and his crowd made up their minds to tell God, "I will not serve!" they were bad from that minute on, forever. They could never even be sorry. They could not bear to stand before God and feel Him looking at them with His clear, kind eyes. They had to find a place to hide. So God made a place for them. We call it Hell. Everyone in Hell is full of hate. The bad angels who live there are called devils.

MICHAEL and the good Angels are now with God in Heaven, God's home. They had passed their test and could see God, the Blessed Trinity. They bowed low before God and sang beautiful songs. They loved God and they loved one another. They were *so very* glad with the happiness that God gave them. They were sharing God's happiness. They were seeing the bright and beautiful God. And that is so wonderful, we can't even imagine what it is like.

GOD MADE different kinds of Angels. He made one special kind to take care of people. He made one Angel for you. Just imagine! God thought of you way back before He had even made the world. He made a big, bright Angel to take care of you while you are little and when you grow big like Mother and Dad. Your Angel will never leave you. God made Angels for all the boys and girls in the whole world. We call these special Angels our Guardian Angels.

NOW BOW your head before God, the Blessed Trinity, just as the Angels do. Close your eyes and talk to God in your soul. He is listening. Whisper, "Thank You, dear God, for making a special Angel to take care of me!"

HAWK AND CHICKENS

This is an outdoor game for any number of players, but it is best played by children who are about the same age and size.

One child is the Hawk, another is Mother Hen, while the rest are the little Chickens.

Mother Hen stands with her arms spread wide. They are her wings. All the children line up behind her in single file, each holding the one in front of him around the waist. The front Chicken holds on to Mother Hen.

The Hawk stands opposite the Hen, and as soon as everyone is lined up, he tries to catch the last Chicken in line. Mother Hen tries to protect her own. Flapping her *wings* and getting in the Hawk's way, she prevents him from reaching the end of the line. Of course, all the Chickens have to follow her as she moves around. If anyone is not watching or is too slow, the line will break and the Hawk will get the last little Chicken. Then a new Hen and a new Hawk are chosen, till everyone has had a turn.

The Speedy FAMILY

So fast runs the Mr.,
His heel gets a blister.

His wife, the Mrs.,
Runs so fast she whizzes.

Their little Miss
Runs as fast as this,

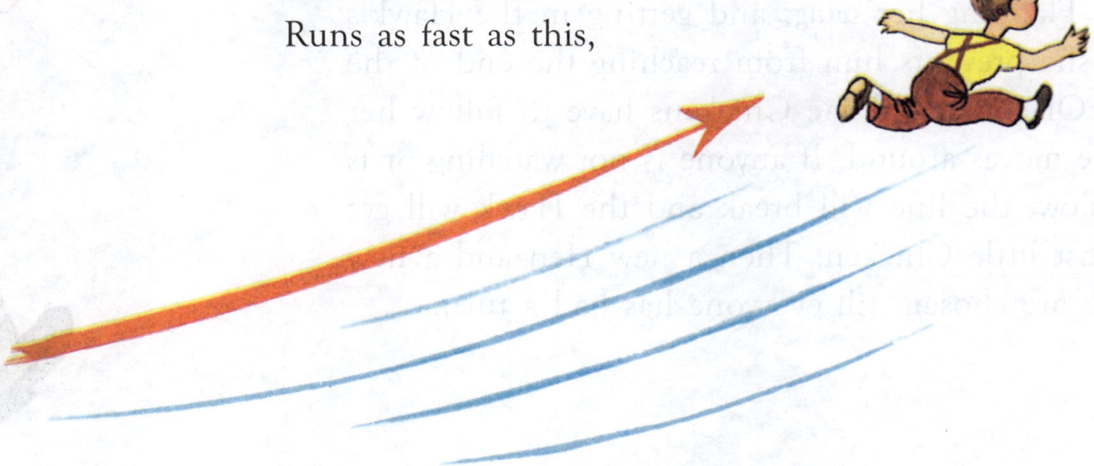

But the little Master
Can run even faster.

GRANDFATHER'S BOWL

(Retold, from Grimm's Fairy Tales)

Once upon a time there was a young man who lived with his wife and their little son. They had a small home of their own. They had enough clothes and enough to eat. Perhaps some day they would even have a car. The young woman kept the house neat and clean. She took good care of all their things while her husband was at work. They were a very happy family.

Oh, I forgot to tell you that the little boy's grandfather lived with them too. He was too old to live by himself, so his son had taken him into his home. The old man's eyes had grown weak with age, so he could not see very well. He got tired easily. When he walked, he moved very, very slowly. His hands, too, were a little shaky, so that he often dropped things by mistake.

When he was a young man, Grandfather had been strong and healthy. He had had a happy family himself. He had worked hard and he had known many things. All his neighbors loved him because he was so gay and kind. Now most of Grandfather's old friends were dead and he would have been a very lonely man if it had not been for his grandchild. Grandfather told him the most wonderful stories. He taught him many things, and the little boy loved to hear Grandfather's rumbling laughter when he played with him and told him of days gone by.

When the little boy's father and mother were around, Grandfather laughed very little. He sat quietly in his chair in the corner and smoked his pipe. Sometimes he fell asleep. Often he looked sad. Why did he look sad? Because, you see, the young man and his wife were impatient with Grandfather. When they went for a walk they

did not take him along because he walked so slowly and got tired so easily. The young man never told his father about his work because sometimes the old man forgot the things he had heard or got them all mixed up. The young woman got upset when Grandfather spilled tobacco on her clean rug. She was angry when he did not hear the doorbell while she was busy cleaning the house. She also complained bitterly about the way Grandfather ate.

"I cannot stand it any longer!" she told her husband one morning. "Grandfather spills the soup all over my clean tablecloth. Only yesterday he broke one of my favorite plates again! Really, if I have to watch that old man eat at my table any longer, I shall leave the house myself."

"I know what you mean," said the young man. "I, myself, feel ashamed to bring guests to our house because of Grandfather. But what can we do? He is my father, and I cannot send him away."

"Leave that to me," answered his wife. "I will go to town

and buy a cheap, wooden bowl and spoon. Grandfather will eat in the kitchen from now on. Then we can have friends here for dinner again, and I shall not have to worry about my china."

And so it happened. From that day on, Grandfather ate alone in the kitchen from his big wooden bowl, and the young people could have guests again without feeling embarrassed. Grandfather did not complain, but he had forgotten all his stories, and even the little boy did not hear him laugh any more.

One night when the young man came home from his work, he found his little boy in the kitchen, whittling a piece of wood. The young woman was at the stove, cooking.

"You look busy, son, what are you making?" the young father asked gaily.

"I am making a bowl for you and Mother to use when you are old and have to eat in the kitchen like Grandfather," replied the little boy.

The young man and his wife looked at each other, and then tears came to their eyes. Suddenly they understood how cruel they had been. And since they were good people, they felt very sorry for what they had done.

From that day on, Grandfather had the place of honor at the table. When it was a nice day, the young man took him for a walk and talked to him about his work. The young woman never again grumbled about spilled food on her table or tobacco on her rugs. She always answered the doorbell quickly, so that Grandfather would not have to get up from his chair.

Grandfather remembered all his stories again. They were more beautiful than they had ever been. Even the guests enjoyed them. And everyone in the house loved to hear Grandfather's gay and rumbling laughter. Yes, they really were a very happy family!

how would you play If you had no toys or games or books

Once when I was little, I was sick for a long time. When you are sick and are not allowed to sit up, there aren't many things you can do. And one gets tired of looking at books all the time.

I was always very fond of songs and verses—everything that rhymed—and while I was lying in bed, I tried to remember as many verses as I could. Then I used them for playing a game with my fingers. It went like this:

I imagined that every finger of my left hand was a particular person I liked. I pretended I had invited them to a party and now we were playing games together. I said the rhymes I remembered, tapping one of my "friends" with each syllable . . . you know, the way you count out to see who is "it"! The finger who got the last beat of the verse was out. And so the game went on with a new verse, until only the winner was left.

Another way to play was to use the fingers of both hands and to beat their tips together while saying the rhyme. I started with my thumbs, then my index fingers, the middle fingers, ring fingers, and at last the pinkies. Then back to the ring fingers, middle fingers and so on, to see which pair got the last beat. They were the winners.

One can also play this game with just one verse, starting it very slowly, then saying it faster and faster, without missing a beat. That takes practice. But when you are good at it, you can do it while saying the words only in your mind. Then you will be able to hear the pretty rhythms your fingers beat, a different one for every poem!